Autistic Ollie

by

Jacob Drum

and

Kit Rees

Autistic Ollie

Author: Jacob Drum

Illustrator: Kit Rees

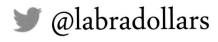 @labradollars

www.kitrees.com

ISBN: 9 781727 493726

First printing: 2018

Autistic Ollie

to all my neuro-siblings...

My mommy says I have a wonderful mind
full of magical powers I'm certain to find.

I sometimes suspect that they're hiding too well,
so I've asked for a hint but nobody will tell.

I write like a chicken, my teacher would say,
but that sounds quite amazing to me anyway.

My hands won't be quiet, my feet won't be still,
which makes some people mad, but I think it's a skill.

I get really nervous and scared in a crowd,
there are strangers too close and it's all very loud.

I always feel better as soon as we're home,
and I play with my toys in my room all alone.

I started to think that perhaps I could fly,
but then Mommy convinced me that I shouldn't try.

I thought that my skill might be crossing the road,
but it made Mommy cry, and it frightened my toad.

Some people say math or computers or cooking, but none of them fit me, and really I'm looking!

I've thought about this, and I've looked into that,
but I can't write a novel and can't swing a bat!

But then I remember the thing that I do,
and what no one can ever do better than you!

I'm awesome at being the person I am,
and you ought to be you because no one else can!

I like when each dinner's the same as before;
it's delicious each day, and I never get bored!

I like to count tiles and to measure each side,
with my tape measure ready I ramble with pride!

My plushies are wonderful, fuzzy, and cute;
and they always want hugs when I'm wanting them, too

My kitty's adorable, silly, and sweet;
when she purrs on my forearms, I stim with my feet!

There's so many skills that a person would need;
there are so many talents to just being me!

I marvel at times, since the odds are so small,
that I have the good fortune of having them all!

So if there's a magical power to find,
I believe that I will! I have plenty of time!

But even if this is the best I can be
I'm not sad or upset, since I like being me!

Thank you for letting Ollie tell you about himself!

Ollie would love to learn a little about you, too...

Ollie loves his plush toys.
What are your favorite toys?

Ollie loves cats.
What is your favorite animal?

Ollie loves to measure things.
What makes you happy?

Ollie is trying to write a story about penguins.

What would you write a story about?

When Ollie is feeling overwhelmed, his toy train helps him to relax. What helps you feel better when you are upset?

Thank You!

Made in the USA
Monee, IL
06 November 2020